WILLIAM WALLBERSON'S WISHES

Natalie Denton

Cover design by: Dani Dixon (www.danidixondesign.co.uk)

To my wonderful husband Jon and two amazing boys Elliot and Cody, who I love more than everything else in the whole wide world.

Jon thank you for always believing in me, especially when I didn't and for buying me two laptops so I could achieve my dreams (the first becoming obsolete because it took me so long to work up the nerve to finally do this).

Elliot thank you for your endless positivity, huge heart and belief in me to write you a book. This book is for you. Thank you also for repeatedly nagging me (in the most loveliest of ways) to get on and finish it - sorry it took so long.

Cody thank you for your crazy antics, hilarious moments and always-welcome hugs that brighten mine and everyone's day. Being able to make you laugh with this book gave me the confidence to finally publish it. Thank you my little one.

CONTENTS

PROLOGUE

'EVERYONE GET DOWN ON THE FLOOR NOW!' The masked bank robber yelled, waving his gun in the air.

William froze.

Boys like William did as they were told.

Boys like William weren't brave.

Boys like William did nothing.

But other boys like William didn't have magic gemstones that made all their wishes come true…

CHAPTER 1

A Parcel Arrives

If one person, just one person, was to notice William Wallberson it would have made his day, no - his week, no - who was he kidding - his year, maybe even all ten of the years he'd been alive.

The problem was no one ever noticed him; not his family, not his teachers, not even the moody school librarian who'd have noticed a mouse sneeze.

The reason for this, William had decided after much internal debate, was that he was just too unremarkable. In fact saying he was unremarkable was like saying the sky was rather blue or that sharks were a bit toothy, it was just a fact, plain and simple. Unlike some boys and girls you might know, William wasn't one to stand out in a crowd. Far from it in fact, he was an average height and an average build for a typical 10-year-old boy, his hair was an average shade of brown and his face was so average that you'd find it hard to remember what he looked like ten seconds after meeting him.

Now you might say, 'well, looks aren't everything, perhaps he has a winning personality!' Well, that's a nice enough thought and all, but sadly not the case here. Don't get it wrong, he wasn't a bad boy, a naughty boy or even a stinky boy; he was just simply a quiet boy. A thinker rather than a talker. A sit-back-and-watcher, rather than a get-up-and-doer. He was neither super smart nor especially thick. People would have said he was nice enough once you get to know him, but that was just it, no one bothered to get to know him. He had zero friends, but zero enemies. Ultimately, he was just someone people passed in the playground without a second thought.

So you're probably thinking, 'wow this is a cheery story... not', but wait! Things are about to change for William, and change in the most fantastic and incredible way, and it all happened one optimistically sunny day in the middle of winter when William returned home from school.

Before he had even stepped in the front door William could hear his two older twin-sisters, Faye and May, arguing as they always did about the same boy they wanted to smooch. Once inside he pulled off the red hand-me-down woolly hat that made his hair stick up on end with static, a seen-better-days brown coat, and his dad's old, but still snuggly soft red scarf and hung them in the hallway. In the living room, his younger brother Kevin was singing 'Row, Row, Row Your Boat' very badly indeed at the top of his voice, much like a cat screeching when you accidentally step on its tail, but worse, much worse. Now baby Brian was awake and screaming like an unstoppable fire alarm, so loud it made William want to shove mash potato into his ear holes. Now mum was shouting at Kevin for waking the baby. *Just a typical afternoon in the Wallberson household,* thought William as he sloped off up to his bedroom unnoticed.

With nothing else to do but homework, he tugged his schoolbooks out of his rucksack and climbed onto the top bunk, where there it was, sitting all by itself; a small, square parcel. A parcel just for him. It had his name and address on it and everything.

Who in the world had sent it? What in the world could be inside it? He wondered, excitement swirling in his brain and belly.

William couldn't remember the last time he got so much as a Christmas card, and yet, here and now, today, there was a parcel just for him, right here on his bed! With a racing heart he ripped it open and turned it upside down where out plopped an oval-shaped purple stone, as well as a letter written in particularly curly-whirly writing.

William my dear boy!

How the good golly gosh are you?

Well would you believe it I'm writing to you from deep within the Amazon?! No, not the online shopping store! The rainforest in South America! I've been living in a very remote place with some splendid indigenous folk for almost a year now. I'm hoping to learn a thing or two from their very talented Shaman, he's a bit of a celebrity in these parts you know!

Anyway you're probably wondering why I've decided to write to you; well I'll tell you. The other day was the Shaman's birthday party, and I was asked to perform a few of my tricks. Well, I did the tree frog out of the hat trick (sadly no rabbits round these parts) and my ever-so-long hankie from the sleeve bit, which both went down very well let me tell you, but in the midst of my juggling with water balloons act I actually dropped one - SPLAT - right on the Chief's youngest grandson! Just when I thought I was going to be in big doo doo with all my new friends, the young lad stood up and got right into it, pretending it was all part of the act! A jolly good sport I can tell you - and my goodness what charisma! What showmanship! Everyone was utterly mesmerised by him.

After the show we had a little chat, this boy and I, and I explained that I had a grandson, that's you William, that was his age, but revealed that unlike him, you are, how do I put this without causing offence, well you're... a tad dull, a bit wallpaper like, more like a ghost than an actual person. So I asked him how he came to be so confident, thinking perhaps I could pass a tip or two onto you. Well then, he said it was all because of a gemstone, a gemstone he says has been in his family for generations! Mysterious is it not?! Well I thought you might need it more than him, so I won it off him in a game of snap, so now it's yours. He tried to tell

me something else about it, but to be honest with you I've only picked
up bits and bobs of the language so far and I'm not 100% sure what he
was trying to tell me about it. I can say 'please', 'thank you very much
indeed', and ask where the library is, but that's about it. But have no
fear my dear boy, I'm sure it's nothing important, but if it is I'll let you
know next time, assuming my fluency has improved by then of course!

All the best
The Magnificently Marvellous Marvellio!!!
(AKA Grandpa Rupert)

William felt lucky if he got a Christmas present from Santa, so a gift like this, one that came smack bang right out of the blue, was completely unheard of. William picked up the stone and turned it over. It was as smooth as any of his marbles, and just as cold, and he liked how it twinkled when he moved it in the light, as though it was almost sparkling. He was just deciding where to keep it when Kevin stormed into their room like an angry tornado of noise and a waterfall of bogies. This happened every day around 4.15pm, exactly five minutes after snuffling up two chocolate biscuits (his one, as well as Baby Brian's) and a giant glass of orange squash.

'NEE-NAW-NEE-NAW' Kevin wailed half running, half spinning in circles, 'I'M AN AM-BAL-ANCE. NEE-NAW-NEE-NAW', ploughing face first into the wardrobe. Laughing like a loony, he got up off the floor and did it again and again and again. Normally at this point

William would wish with all his might that Kevin would be quiet because he was trying to do his homework, but Kevin would always carry on being the oddball that he was, no matter how noisily William huffed and puffed.

'Kevin can you go and do that somewhere else please,' William muttered quietly to himself as he turned the gemstone over in his fingers, fully expecting Kevin to just carry on giving himself a head injury as though it was his life's mission. 'Like in next door's wheelie bin for example?'

Just then something remarkable happened. Kevin actually stopped. He stopped moving, stopped nee-nawing, stopped head-butting the furniture and looked up at his older brother as if seeing him for the first time. He smiled and said, 'okay William' and left the room.

What the cheese and pickle sandwich just happened? Thought William, his mind racing with confusion. It was as if the world had flipped on its head and everyone decided to talk like robots. This was unheard of! This was insane! This was unbelievable! Kevin actually did something he was told for once! That had never, ever happened in the entire time he'd been alive. *This is crazy!*

No, William thought suddenly, staring at the gemstone which had begun to make his palm hot; *this is magic!*

CHAPTER 2

Chicken Surprise

No way, thought William, *there's just no way magic is real, it's just not possible!*

But Kevin had NEVER EVER listened to William before, never ever ever, not even when his life depended on it. There was the time William told Kevin not to touch the electric fence at the zoo, he totally ignored him and wound up having hair all pointy like a hedgehog for two whole weeks. There was the time Kevin decided to put Faye and May's hamster 'Nibbler' down his pants, which ended up in yet another trip to the hospital. And perhaps worst of all there was the time William had tried to explain to Kevin that the brown stuff in Baby Brian's nappy wasn't chocolate. Yet as William looked out of his bedroom window he could see Kevin climbing onto the neighbour's wall and prising open the wheelie bin lid.

Could it be magic? William wondered rolling the shiny stone in his palm.

'Dinnnnnnneeeeerrrr!' Mum yelled from downstairs.

William's nose wrinkled in disgust as he stepped out onto the landing. Wednesday... Chicken Surprise. Now it's not that William was an ungrateful child, he'd eat whatever his mum put in front of him because he didn't want to cause a fuss. It's just that his mum wasn't a good cook, at all, she was terrible in fact, the worst of the worst, rotten pants would taste better than the meals she cooked. Kevin's four-day-old rotten pants at that. But it wasn't her fault. When she was little her big sister bet her 50p that she couldn't eat four packets of Fizwig's Furiously Fizzy Feasts in one go. Well she did, and she won the bet, but afterwards she had zero taste buds left. Not one. So all food tastes the same to her. It tastes like nothing. No flavour at all. So every night ends up being a 'surprise night', meaning William's mum would just throw together what-ever she found in the cupboards and call it a 'surprise'. The only real surprise was that they never ended up in hospital!

Monday is fish surprise, Tuesday's pork surprise, Thursday's beef surprise, Friday's broccoli surprise (usually the worst), and Satur-day is pasta surprise. Now Sunday can either be the best day of the week or the worst, it all depends on what she finds, because Sunday is 'tin can surprise', where she'll select two or three cans at random from the back of the cupboard, throw them together in a bowl, mix them up, pop them in the microwave and hope for the best. Dishes like "baked beans a la custard" or "hot-dog and rice-pudding delight", both of which weren't actually too bad surprisingly, unlike "pilchard and fruit-salad stew", which had hands down been the worst by far.

Sat at the table William and his sisters gloomily looked over the contents of their steaming bowls of grim brown mush, even baby Brian wasn't sure and William had once seen him eat half a shoe.

'What's in it Mum?' Faye asked tentatively.

'Chicken and er, some bits and bobs,' Mum replied absent-mindedly as she scrubbed away at the dirty pans in the sink. 'See if you can guess!'

'I'm frightened to,' May whispered to her twin who nodded in agreement.

She's a mad woman, thought William, poking the sludge with his spoon, wondering what other kids ate for dinner. Surely not this.

William rubbed the stone in his pocket. What better time to see if this stone really is magic? *Okay, here goes nothing*, William thought nervously. He coughed to clear his throat and then asked very quietly but ever so politely, 'Mm-mum, ppp-please may we have ice cream for dinner instead?'

Silence.

You could hear cars driving in the road, cats wailing in the alleyways, and all the stuff going on inside baby Brian's tummy, but apart from that, nothing. The twins' jaws fell open in unison. Baby Brian stopped whinging, and Mum dropped the bubble-covered ladle back into the washing up bowl with a magnificent *plop!*

It felt like an eternity had passed, but slowly a smile stretched across his mum's face as if it was waking up from a long sleep. It was the biggest smile William could ever remember seeing on her lovely face.

'William! That's a great idea!' She said, heading straight for the freezer.

Faye and May's mouths dropped another inch and their eyes looked as though they might actually pop out of their heads.

'I think we still have some vanilla ice cream left over from Dad's birthday,' she said enthusiastically, digging around in the icy drawers before tugging a snow-encrusted white tub from the frozen grip of the freezer wall. 'Oooh and look what I've found… anyone want sugar snap peas with it?'

William and his sisters smiled but shook their heads frantically.

Scooping out a huge spoonful of the marvellous creamy goodness, William's mum made her way to the table, ready to plop it straight on top of William's brown dinner goo. Acting fast William rubbed the stone and bravely asked, 'mmm-maybe in a separate bowl?'

'Sure sweetie,' she smiled. And that was that. A few seconds later the whole Wallberson family were sitting around the table greedily digging into the best dinner their mum had ever made. Except for Dad of course, and Kevin who was... *oh no* thought William.

BANG, BANG, BANG, came a knock at the front door. Mum jumped up to answer it.

'Oh hello Mrs Patel,' he could hear his mum saying. 'What on Earth!? Oh no I am so sorry. No, I have no idea what he was doing in your bin. No, I didn't know he was in there. Of course I won't let it happen again. I am so sorry. Please say hello to Mr Patel for us. Goodnight Mrs Patel and sorry again!'

Magic, William thought smiling to himself as he gulped down mouthful after mouthful of delicious ice cream, *it had to be magic.*

CHAPTER 3

Mr. Fizzy's Super Duper World of Sweets 'n Stuff

For William, the next day began like every other, but he knew this day would be spectacularly different, because today he had a magic stone! That's what the Chief's grandson must have been trying to tell Grandpa Rupert, he decided as he got himself ready for school. Well William certainly wasn't going to let this opportunity pass him by without some fun!

Everyday on his way to school William passed a sweet shop. It was the most glorious shop in all of Middletown. It was packed to the rafters with every kind of sweet you could possibly ever imagine existing and then a hundred more you hadn't even considered: bon-bons, gummy bears, jelly beans, laces, lollipops, sherbets, boiled sweets, chewy sweets, fizzy sweets, sour sweets, sweets of every shape, size, flavour and colour. It was pure sugary heaven. Now the thing was the Wallbersons didn't have a lot of money to spare on things like sweets, perhaps if it was their birthday or if a relative came to stay they might get a packet to share, but that was it. So you can understand why William was so drawn to *Mr. Fizzy's Super Duper World of Sweets 'n Stuff*. Kids were always pouring in and out of there before and after school but the best William could hope for, was to get a waft of the mouth-watering sugar-rich scent as it escaped through the door when someone went in or out. It was somewhere he had always wanted to go but had never been able to. Until now.

William tucked his shirt in, swept his hair over to the side out of his brown eyes and took a big breath in. *Ok here I go*, he thought, bravely mustering every ounce of courage in his small being.

A little bell jingled cheerily above the door as he stepped inside, while a rush of sweet-smelling warm air greeted him like a big hug. The sight of all those huge jars of different coloured sweets stacked neatly in long rows along dark mahogany shelves made his skin go all goose bumpy in anticipation. It was more incredible than what he'd been able to see through the window. It was like a museum and all the exhibits were edible! His eyes feasted on the awesome sights while his mouth watered uncontrollably. There must have been over 200 jars! How could he possibly choose just one type to try? He'd left early this morning to ensure he'd get to the shop just after it opened in the hope no one from school would see him in case this all went terribly wrong and he looked like a complete chump, but how was he going to choose in time? Moving slowly around the shop William ran a finger across the jars, reading each label aloud, savouring every word as if he was devouring them. 'Crackling Strawberry Jam Clouds. Banana Bubblegum Snowcakes. Cola and Custard Sherbet Straws.' His eyes got bigger and bigger as he studied every jar, imagining what each one might taste like. 'Fizzing Chocolate Unicorn Horns'.

'They're my favourite! They're new you know.'

William spun round half in shock, half in despair. Oh no, no, no! No one was meant to be here so early. There was no way he was going to try out his magic stone now, what if he failed! He'd never get over the embarrassment.

'You don't recognise me do you?' The girl said sadly, looking at the floor. She had hazel eyes and dark brown hair, which she'd tied into pigtails, while her skin was a delicate shade in between. 'I'm Iris Bondy, I'm in your year at school. Mrs. Bloomer's class.'

William was amazed. She, Iris that was, knew who he was. Someone from his school actually knew who he was!

He clutched the stone in his pocket with all his strength, wishing that it might help him to summon the courage to say something that wouldn't be totally lame or eternally embarrassing. It was taking him a while to think of something and Iris, who at first had looked sad, was now looking at him concerned as though William was turning a different colour or growing an extra head or something. *It's now or never,* he decided. 'H-h-h-hello Iris, I'm Will – William,' he stammered shyly. 'I know who you are.'

'Oh great,' she beamed, scratching the side of her nose. She had a tooth missing but William thought she still had a pretty smile. 'So what are you going to choose?'

'I, um, I-I don't know…' was all William could manage, still overwhelmed by the vast choice of treats.

'Can I help you?' Came a shrill voice from behind the till, 'this isn't a library you know. If you're not buying then move along.' The tall thin woman, who had a face like a pelican, said sternly at William, scowling at him as if he were up to no good.

William panicked, what was he going to do? If he left now Iris might tell everyone at school he was a complete weirdo who'd rather look at sweets than eat them, or worse that he couldn't afford them. But if he tried to use his magic stone and it didn't work, he'd look like an even bigger wally.

'That's alright Marion,' a gentle voice stirred from behind a row of shelves. 'I've got this.'

Marion huffed and stropped off to dust a row of jars angrily with a pink feather duster.

'That's Mr Fizzy,' Iris whispered in William's ear, as a smartly dressed old man appeared with a huge welcoming smile on his round, wrinkled face that made his eyes crinkle and twinkle.

William looked at him in complete awe, it was like meeting the Queen, only cooler and even more impressive. More like meeting an astronaut footballer who had his own YouTube channel and who was also related to Father Christmas!

Although he'd never actually met Mr. Fizzy before, he looked exactly as William had imagined. William guessed he was around 100 but couldn't be sure as all old people looked the same. Perched on the end of Mr. Fizzy's chubby red nose was a pair of half-moon spectacles, while his bald head was flanked with little white wisps of fluffy hair just above his ears, that looked so much like candy floss William wondered if it actually was. He wasn't much taller than they were but was quite round, and wore a crisp white shirt with purple bow tie, navy blue trousers, and smart maroon velvet waistcoat that looked as though it was struggling a little to remain fastened.

'Hel-llo,' William gulped.

'Fizzy Chocolate Unicorn Horns, a great choice,' Mr Fizzy said with a warm smile, 'but have you tried these yet?'

He rolled a wooden ladder which was lent up against the sweet shelves that lined the wall, a yard or two across and carefully climbed the rungs, stopping at the sixth shelf to remove a jar of pink, white, blue and yellow. The label read "BIRTHDAY CAKE MALLOWSQUEAKS".

William shook his head, not able to tear his eyes away from the pretty marbled balls inside. 'I've never actually been *in* here before Sir,' he managed, gripping the stone tightly in his pocket for support.

'Oh my word,' Mr Fizzy sounded startled. 'Well then you must try some, on the house of course!' And with that he shuffled off to the counter where he emptied a large scoop into a red and white striped paper bag and happily handed it to William who just couldn't believe his luck! He felt almost dizzy with excitement and relief.

'Thank you! Thank you so much!' He finally managed. He was so intoxicated with the rush of success that before he knew what he was saying words rushed out of his mouth, 'Um, Mr. Fizzy?!' He almost shouted, unable to contain his excitement, all the while revolving the stone in his pocket. 'Would my ffr-friend Iris, well might she be able to have some too p-please? But only if that's okay and not too rude.' His voice trailing off to a whisper by the end as his nerves got the better of him.

Mr. Fizzy looked at the two of them in surprise and then with a little chuckle and a wink at the girl said, 'well of course! Iris is my favourite customer after all!'

Iris let out a little sneeze, followed by a giggle, 'oops,' she laughed, her cheeks reddening. 'That happens when I get excited.'

This made William like Iris even more. But they didn't talk to each other all the way to school. No, not because they'd fallen out, it was because they were too busy enjoying their mallowsqueaks too much. They were *that* good they didn't want to talk or do anything other than cherish every single second enjoying the taste explosion in their mouths. Each one was exactly how William imagined a party to taste, not that he'd ever been invited to one. The balls were smooth and hard like marbles on the outside, but once you'd sucked the birthday cake icing-like flavour off, you could crunch through the sugary shell to find a burst of fizzy sherbet strawberry marshmallow that seemed to dance on the tongue and sing to the taste buds. His mouth had never felt more alive, and neither had he. Today was going to be the best day ever!

CHAPTER 4

The Mad Ox

Today is going to be the worst day ever! William realised, paralysed with fear as he stared into the demented eyes of the school bully Maddox Bullburn who at any moment was likely to unleash an untameable rage that might see him rip William's arm from its socket or punch him in the eye.

Maddox, or The Mad Ox as he was known by everyone who feared him at Middletown Primary School, including the teachers, was as wide as he was tall. Imagine if you will, an overinflated beach ball with podgy arms and legs sticking out of the sides that look like the sweaty tubes of meat you often see revolving in kebab shop windows, and that's The Mad Ox. His pink moon face would often make people think of gammon, while his snub nose and constantly downturned mouth gave him the look of someone who's face had got stuck doing an impression of an unhappy pug. His hair was jet black and his beady eyes, not to mention his soul, were as dark to match. Although Maddox was in the year above William, everyone knew who he was, and more importantly, knew to avoid him.

The unfortunate situation William now found himself in, had arisen that morning as Iris and William neared the school gates. True to form Maddox was picking on a child, today it happened to be a small boy from year 4. Nothing unusual there. Another day, another victim. Ordinarily William would have just kept his head down, not looked in Maddox's direction and made it into school alive. A survival tactic that had worked thus far, because to this day Maddox, much like the rest of his school, hadn't noticed William existed. But today was different. Today he had someone with him, someone who had noticed him. Could he call her a friend yet? Either way, walking past the school's equivalent of The Minotaur was sure to be harder than normal. He told himself that if he could just keep his head low and his feet fast they'd be alright...

'Oi! Mad Ox, leave that kid alone,' Iris bellowed bravely.

Oh great, William thought to himself as panic took hold, *I had to go befriend the only person in the whole universe who wants to stand up to Maddox the Mad Ox! Nice one William.*

'Iris, what are you doing?!' William whispered out of the side of his mouth, tugging on her elbow to draw her away, but it was no good, she had rooted herself to the spot a few metres from the quickly reddening Ox.

'What did you say?' he spat, unconsciously releasing the younger boy's collar from his doughy hand.

Like a mouse freed from the grip of a hungry snake, the quivering year 4 fell to the ground, hastily scooped up his things and scurried away as fast as the wind, only pausing briefly to squeak a hurried 'thank you' in the direction of his would-be heroes.

'I said leave that boy alone, which you have done now so we will be on our way,' Iris remarked with a nod of her head, 'good day to you.'

She's completely bonkers and she's going to get us killed, was all William could think.

Maddox began laughing. Not a cute or contagious sort of laugh, rather a slow, guttural laugh from a nightmare, like one a hairy monster pig or scary clown might make before it starts chasing you. 'Oh you're going to get it now loser,' he muttered, punching a clenched fist into his palm with a menacing look that made William want to run away very, very fast.

'Oh yeah?' Iris took a big step towards him, chin raised in defiance.

'Yeah!' Maddox moved closer, so close William was sure Iris must be able to feel the steam radiating off his sweaty red face.

'Oh yeah?'

'Yeah!'

'Oh yeah?'

'Yea…'

'Okay I think we should probably get going,' William said in his softest voice in the hope he wouldn't rile Maddox up or disappoint Iris, by sounding too bossy or too scared. 'The bell is probably about to ring and we don't want to be late.'

'And who's this?' Maddox said, as if suddenly noticing William. 'Your boyfriend?'

'His name is William Wallberson, and he knows karate, tai-kwon-do, kick-boxing, Brazilian Jiu Jitsu, and has a knockout punch that is so hard that if he were to hit you in the mouth you'd be eating your packed lunch with your bottom for weeks!'

'What?' Maddox was clearly confused.

Iris sighed impatiently while shifting her weight to the other foot, 'because your teeth would go all the way down to your bum, dummy!'

Maddox scratched his head, 'what's a Bum Dummy?'

'Iris,' William whispered out the corner of his mouth. 'I think you've got me confused with someone else.' He didn't even know what Brazilian Jiu Jitsu was! Was it a type of drink? But there was no time to find out because Iris' bulging eyes, almost out of their sockets, made him realise she must have a plan up her sleeve. 'Oooooh yeah, I do, I mean I most definitely do know Brazilian Judo Juice and trust me, you don't want me to unleash it on you,' William said bravely, dramatically throwing his hands up into a karate chop pose.

'Oh yeah?' Maddox snarled again, but this time less confidently.

'Yeah!' Iris retaliated.

'Oh ye...'

'Yes I think we are all in agreement here,' William interrupted, sure of where this was going - a dozen more 'yeahs' and 'oh yeahs' - plus he was eager to end this situation and get into school before the bell rang.

The bell rang.

'Maddox Bullburn! Iris Bondy! And, and, um er, you, thingy,' the school's headmaster, Mr. Creedicorn loomed up behind them like a giant rain cloud. He was short for a grown up, and his belly stuck out so far that when he turned a corner, you saw it before you saw the rest of him. His face was long and looked like a giant thumb, and it was almost always mauve. Tufts of grey hair sprouted from his nostrils and ears, but he had little of it left on his head. Just a thin wispy white crescent he'd pasted from one side over to the other. His glasses were rectangular and thin, and always seemed to be steamed up like a window. 'Um, I want to say Walter is it? Or maybe Nathan? Jasper perhaps? No, no I know it's Marcus, it's Marcus isn't it?'

'It's Will-William sir,' William said, trying not to shake.

'Yes I was about to say that if you had given me one more second to think. William. William. William Woolly? No that's not it. William Woowooworm? No, that's not even a name!' He shouted, arguing with himself.

'It's Wallberson, sir. William Wallberson.'

'Yes yes I knew that! Of course I knew that!' he screamed so loud and trembled with so much anger that his hair wisps freed themselves from the left side of his head and floated up in the wind, making it appear as though they were waving. His face was now a magnificent shade of beetroot purple, while his glasses were so fogged up, small beads of condensation had formed on the inside.

William clenched the stone in his pocket with all his might, praying he and Iris wouldn't get in trouble. Just then, miraculously the school's secretary shouted out of the reception door. 'Mr. Creedi-corn, it's happened again! This time in the girls' toilets on the second floor. Poo everywhere!'

'Oh. For. Goodness. Sake!' Creedicorn raged. 'You three! Get to your class before I put you all in detention.'

'This isn't over,' Maddox growled in a disturbingly low voice for an eleven year old as he peeled off towards the Year 6 classrooms, 'and now I know your names, you're on *The List*.'

CHAPTER 5

The Fight

William hadn't taken in one word Mrs. Plumpton, his teacher, had said about the Ancient Egyptians that morning. All he could think about were all the different ways Maddox might physically harm him at play time; head down the toilet, atomic wedgie, knuckle sandwich in the privates… all the things he'd seen on TV but had never had the misfortune of experiencing himself. Why, oh why did his one and only friend have to pick a fight with the school's one and only bully? Now they were both on 'The List' and that meant only one thing… certain doom.

The bell for break cut through his thoughts like a guillotine. As his classmates poured into the playground, William peered round the door from the safety of the cloakroom. *Perhaps I could just stay in here,* he thought, *no one would notice me*, and with that backed into the wall and pulled some coats that were hanging to the left and right of him over his face and body so that only his legs and feet were poking out. But then he remembered Iris. He'd never forgive himself if Maddox hurt her. After all it was partly his fault that they were on his list, wasn't it? After a little to-ing and fro-ing William decided that he couldn't hide in the cloakroom forever. That was the old William, and as of yesterday, he became the new, brave version; William 2.0. So while rubbing his lucky stone once more, he began weighing up his options.

'Oh! Who is that in there?' William heard the startled voice of Mrs Plumpton, who began stripping back the coats he'd hidden himself behind. 'Oh, it's you, Wesley.'

'William.'

'Of course, William. Silly me. Right then off you go, go get some fresh air,' she began humming to herself as she shooed him out of the doorway, seemingly oblivious to his resistance as he dug his heels in. With one rather abrupt shove he was outside, vulnerable and alone, like a rehabilitated zoo animal released back into the wild. Before he could argue, explain or beg, the classroom door was closed swiftly behind him, and no less than ten feet away, Maddox stood like a crazed animal ready to pounce on his prey. One slow step at a time he began moving his bulk towards William, who had decided closing his eyes would maybe make it all somehow go away, or at the very least, mean the punches that were sure to rain down on him, hurt less. He dug his hands deep into his pockets, clutching the cold stone for support, wishing with all his might for a miracle.

William's heart raced, his mind even more so trying to quickly think up a plan to get himself out of this predicament. He knew Maddox was close now because he could hear his heavy panting and smell his cheesy crisp breath.

'Oww, what was that?!' Maddox yelped in pain.

William's eyes shot open to witness Maddox in a heap on the floor, cradling the top of his head with both arms. When he finally did lift his head, William could see the confusion in his eyes, but there was something else there too, was it fear? Someone or something must have hit him, or maybe a seagull dropped a rock or maybe a bee had stung him? Whatever it was William was grateful for the intervention, even if it only gave him a couple of extra minutes to live. But as William met Maddox's eyes, something unheard of happened, and all the kids in the playground who were gathering round, saw it too. Maddox was crying. The school bully, who had made so many kids' lives miserable, who seemingly hurt and wounded his fellow pupils on a random rotation without so much as a second thought, was now himself the victim of such an attack, and for once, got to feel what it's like to be on the receiving end.

Snot began gushing from his snubby nose joined by streams of salty tears that streaked his pudgy face. 'Ow! That really hurt!'

At first it started with a quiet titter from one of the kids who had heard Maddox's yelp. Then a couple of others who could no longer suppress their giggles joined in. Then just a few seconds after that, it seemed like the entire circle of onlookers were bent over double, laughing and pointing at the school's biggest meanie-pants who had been reduced to a blubbering mess, wailing in giant sobs that shook his big belly like a bowl full of jelly.

'Shut it,' he screamed at them, fists clenched. 'Shut up, or, or, or I'm telling my mummy!'

But this drastic transformation of character was just too funny, in the matter of seconds Maddox the Menace had gone from scary to snivelling, and the children couldn't help themselves, they were falling about with laughter left and right, which only made Maddox cry even harder, sending him off squealing in the direction of the boys' toilets, wailing 'Mummmmmmmmmmmy!' at the top of his lungs.

'What did I miss?' Iris asked nonchalantly as she skipped over to William, a big smile on her face.

'I'm not s-sure,' William managed totally agog. 'One minute Maddox was coming towards me, I was sure my life was over, and the next he was standing there, bawling like a baby.'

'He did it!' A boy in year 5 shouted pointing at William.

Oh no, William panicked, *no, no I didn't do anything. Did I?*

'Yeah, he did it, that boy there,' a little girl with enormously long pigtails in year 2 chimed in.

'That's William, he's in my class,' piped up Graham Lewis, the cleverest and most popular boy in the whole school. William's mouth fell open, *Graham Lewis knows my name!* He thought mesmerised as Graham walked towards him and put an arm around his shoulder, 'three cheers for William the Conqueror, hip hip...'

'Hooray!' came a resounding cheer from the ever increasing circle of children from all years of the school.

'Hip, hip!' Graham continued.

'No, no, I didn't...' William tried to protest to no avail as the chants grew louder and louder.

'Hooray!' The crowd rallied, growing bigger by the minute, words spreading eagerly from lips to ears.

'Hip, hip!' Graham had whipped the children into a real frenzy now, as it seemed the whole school was crowded round William, grinning and cheering in unison with their hands punching the air.

'Hooray!' They sang.

'And one for luck!' Iris shouted, raising William's arm high in the air.

'Hooray!'

And just like a starting gun being fired to begin a race, the final 'hooray' was all the children needed to surge forward to congratulate their hero. Some shook his hand or clapped him on the back. Shy ones waved and gave a friendly thumbs up, while brave ones moved in for chest-squeezing hugs. One kid gave him a Wagon Wheel and another her half eaten packet of Prawn Cocktail crisps. An older girl William couldn't remember seeing before planted a quick kiss on his cheek, which immediately made him blush, and a boy in his class who played for the local football team's under 12 squad, invited him for a kickabout on the weekend. He had never experienced such attention in all his life and as much as he was glad to finally be noticed, he found it overwhelming. He couldn't speak, only nod and smile. By the time the bell rang William felt as though he'd run a marathon, uphill, backwards, and through honey, he was utterly exhausted! He let out a huge breath, dropped his head low and clung to the wall behind him for support.

'Wow, my friend the warrior!' Iris beamed, bending over to join him so she could see his face. 'You'll go down in Middletown Primary history for this!'

'No! Please! It really wasn't like that. I didn't do anything,' William panted.

'Yeah right William, you can't fool me, you're just being modest. You took down the school bully all by yourself! I can't wait to see what you do next!'

Neither can I, thought William half scared, half excited.

CHAPTER 6

The Chipped Teapot Cafe

The rest of the school day passed in a blur. Kids slapping him on the back to congratulate him, others wanting to shake his hand, and more than a handful asked for selfies when the teachers weren't watching. William had never felt more alive or more visible. People were noticing him, and more than that, people liked him! He felt unstoppable, but try as he might, he couldn't ignore the icky feeling that rolled around in his stomach like a rotten cabbage. Guilt. Yep that was it. He felt like a fraud. He hadn't stopped Maddox. He didn't do anything except close his eyes and wish for him to go away. So no, he hadn't done anything. Or had he?

Maybe it was the stone, he thought with more hope than reason, as he walked out of school at the end of the day to the applause of hundreds of kids, most of whom even he didn't know. *Why not? Everything else I've wanted so far has happened, so why not that? Maybe I just need to try it again, somewhere away from school and see what happens.*

'There he is!'

The words made William jump what felt like eight feet in the air, as they came like an accusation more than a greeting, but when he turned around relief washed over him as he realised it was just Iris with her signature beaming smile.

'You almost gave me a heart attack!' He puffed nervously.

'Sorry William, it's just I've been looking forward to seeing you. Want to come over to my house for dinner? My Grandad just got me a new video game - *Captain Bubblegum 2: This Time it's Blowable*, have you played it already? Or if you don't like video games, I could teach you some of the magic tricks I've been working on, see there's this one I do with my yoyo, it's like this, see..'

William stopped dead, it was like a celestial beam of light had shone down on him from the heavens. This was the moment he'd waited for forever, ever since he overheard Tommy O'Donnell invite Sam Tucksworth over to his house for an after school playdate in Year 1. Over the years he'd seen every one of his classmates get the chance to go round to a friend's house for dinner and a play. He wished for nothing else for years; every eyelash, every birthday cake candle, that one shooting star he'd seen fly across the sky when his dad had taken him camping - all spent on the hope he'd one day be invited over to a friend's house. William yearned to know what chicken nuggets, fish fingers, burgers, pizza, chips and beans tasted like, and to see what the inside of someone else's home looked like. To be invited was to be accepted, which meant that you're wanted. Yet he knew he couldn't say yes. He had something too important to do, and he knew he had to do it today. He had to know for sure one way or the other whether this stone was really magic or not, and he couldn't risk embarrassing himself in front of what he hoped was his first of many new friends.

'That's in-incredibly nice of you and normally I would have leapt at the chance, but I can't tonight. I'm sorry Iris.'

Iris smiled quickly and looked at the floor, shoving the yoyo back in her pocket, 'that's alright William, I expect you've got lots of new friends now you're famous and all.'

'No, that's not it! I, I, I...' William didn't know what to say. He finally had a real friend and he felt for sure he was about to blow it. He exhaled and looked at the ground, but he couldn't tell her the truth. She might think he was crazy. But he didn't want to lie to her either, so he just stared at his shoes.

'Okay William, see you around,' she sighed, scuttling off to the gates. William's heart sank when he caught sight of her using her sleeve to brush away what he guessed was a tear.

The walk home was rubbish. William felt so awful that he'd upset

Iris, and as if the weather were mimicking his mood, it started to rain. Hard. Icy beads of water smacked against his face and trickled down his collar like frozen spiders, while a cold arctic wind blew angrily with its frosty breath. He wasn't even a third of the way home when the number 55 bus hurtled past him through a lake-like puddle in the road, which sent a wave of dirty water crashing down on top of him, soaking him from top to toe. Even his pants were drenched!

'Figures,' he muttered to himself gloomily and pulled his hat down as far as it would go and his scarf up around his face so high that now only his eyes and nose were poking out. It felt as though the soft wool of the scarf was giving him a much needed hug, even if it was just to his face, it sent a warm glow from his tummy to his finger tips, helping him to feel a little better inside.

Shoving his hands deep into his pockets for warmth he gripped the stone with all his might, but he wasn't sure what to wish for.

Not to be cold and wet would be a start, he decided. He still had a long way to walk home and the rain was really starting to hammer it down.

Over the other side of the road, past the pelican crossing, a neon light flickered above some sort of shop. As William tended to look down when he walked anywhere he realised he'd never noticed it before. Crossing over he stopped just in front of the place and read the electric yellow sign: '*The Chipped Teapot Cafe*'. An upright teapot appeared next to the cafe's name in blue neon light, but would turn off every other second and a teapot pouring liquid into a cup would turn on. It made him smile.

'Ah, that's a nice smile,' a woman said from the cafe's doorway, who was tying up her pink apron with small yellow birds on it, under which she wore ripped jeans and a green wooly jumper. Her hair was blonde and tied into a long plait at the end of which was a blue bow. She had a friendly face covered in freckles, and William decided she was probably around the same age as his mum.

She stepped outside, opening a small lilac umbrella with penguins on it. The penguins also had umbrellas but weren't using them to protect themselves from the rain. Some were battling one another as if their umbrellas were swords, others sat in them like boats, a few were riding them like horses. The whole thing seemed frankly ridiculous to William, first the idea of penguins getting hold of a bunch of umbrellas in Antarctica seemed very unlikely, and second, the likelihood that they would use them in this way seemed a little absurd.

'Coming in?' the cafe lady asked after throwing a black rubbish bag in the big wheelie bin on the street. 'This doesn't show any signs of stopping anytime soon.' She pointed up to the thick, black rain clouds above.

William looked up at the sky. Huge fat wet pellets poked him in the eyes. He wiped the water away with a soggy sleeve and peered into the cafe through the door that she was now holding ajar for him. It looked cosy and warm, while the air seemed to dance with the smell of freshly baked cookies. Before he could think, he found his feet already moving, inside and out of the rain.

It surprised William that there were no customers inside, because The Chipped Teapot Cafe was lovely. Okay so none of the furniture matched and none of it looked new, there were odd paintings on the walls that William could well believe were drawn by a sugar-addled toddler, and over in the corner a leak from the roof dripped rhythmically into a metal bucket. But it was warm, it was homely and the counter was stacked with more cakes, buns, and biscuits than William had ever seen in one place before.

'Awful weather eh?' the cafe lady called as she reappeared from a door that William guessed led to the kitchen. 'How about a nice hot chocolate?'

William suddenly felt hot and panicked, he grabbed the stone and feeling embarrassed managed to mumble, 'I'm so sorry I don't have any money,' and apologetically started backing away towards the door.

'Oh don't you worry about that,' she waved, busily gathering cups and saucers. 'I'll just be glad of the company, not seen a soul all day, and I'm not likely to now with it being like this. No you're alright. Stay and wait for it to pass, have a hot chocolate on me.'

William couldn't believe his luck! That settled it. The stone was definitely magic. Definitely. Dare he try for more?

Edging closer to the counter his eyes found a stack of pink iced doughnuts, jam oozing from the centre. Licking his lips uncontrollably, he felt for the warm stone once more, 'they look nice,' he whispered, more to himself than the cafe lady.

'Oh help yourself! Here, have a plate. Take a couple if you like. Everything on that plate needs eating up today or it'll end up in the bin. Here, take a couple of paper bags too so you can take the extra ones home with you.'

William didn't need telling twice, swiftly taking a bite out of the one with the most icing. He smiled contentedly, imagining the look on his family's faces when he returned home with the rest for them to share. Edging carefully to the nearest table, William set down the leaning tower of sticky baked goods on a small round metal table with little mosaic tiles on top. Not wanting to get any of the chairs wet, he decided to hang his coat up by the door, but when he got there he realised he'd left a trail of puddles behind him. Reaching for his stone, he wondered what he should do, perhaps he'd just sit on the doormat until he'd dried off.

'There you go,' the cafe lady said, handing him a bundle of fabrics. 'They were my son Peter's. He's outgrown those now so feel free to keep them. You can change in the toilet, it's just over there. Here's a towel to get dry and here's a plastic bag to put all your wet stuff in.'

William opened his arms and took a closer look at the pile of clothes he'd been handed. All of it looked brand new, and not only that, it was all the expensive stuff that the cool kids wore that William's family would never have been able to afford unless they won the lottery. There was even a pair of trainers that all the cool kids talked about, and they didn't have a mark on them. William didn't know what to say, it was like Father Christmas himself had just handed him the best gear ever.

'...or you can donate them to a charity shop afterwards if they're not your style, I don't know if they're still "cool" or not. Sorry, maybe I've embarrassed you. I just thought you might like to get dry,' she offered, sensing that maybe William didn't like the clothes and held out her hands to take them back.

'No!' William clung to the clothes in panic. 'I mean, I'm sorry, but no, I mean yes, I mean yes please and t-t-thank you,' he took a deep breath and organised his thoughts then said in a clear, calm voice, 'what I mean is, I would definitely like to keep them. Thank you.'

A relieved smile sprang onto the cafe lady's face, 'oh goody! My Peter is nearly as big as me now, he grows so fast, his clothes barely get worn before I'm buying him new ones. I'm just glad they'll get some more use,' she called, heading back to the kitchen behind the counter. Once there William heard the unmistakable sound of whipped cream being squirted from a can. 'Marshmallows and a chocolate flake?' she asked, popping her head around the door.

All William could do at this point was smile and nod, and hope he wasn't drooling.

Magic is real, he decided once and for all.

CHAPTER 7

Trouble in town

The next morning was a beautiful winter's day. Even though the air was cold and thick with the promise of snow, the sun was bright and warm. Jack Frost had been busy overnight, stencilling crystals onto everything in sight including the pavement which felt very slippy underfoot. Today was mufti day, a day most children look forward to with excitement, but traditionally a huge source of worry for William, as his wardrobe only contained hand-me-down girls shirts from Faye and May and taken in and turned up trousers that his dad wore in the olden days of the 1990s'. Normally, no one would have noticed him whatever he wore so he had always supposed it didn't really matter what he looked like, but now he was the brave vanquisher of the demon dragon Maddox, and surely everyone would definitely notice him today. But this mufti day would be very different from all those that had come before it, because thanks to Cafe Lady, he was decked out, top to toe in the best clothes imaginable and everything fitted him perfectly.

'Wow are they Flame Treds?' Graham Lewis was almost falling over himself to get a look at William's gleaming white trainers. 'My mum said they are impossible to get!'

'Oh these?' William answered awkwardly once the shock of realising Graham was not only talking to him, but had started walking with him in the direction of school too. 'Oh um, maybe, I can't remember.'

'They're sick!'

'Right, yes, sick,' William managed once he'd composed himself.

As they approached *Mr. Fizzy's Super Duper World of Sweets 'n Stuff*, William was aware of a group of boys from his year staring at him. He wasn't used to people staring and he couldn't help but feel a little uncomfortable. Forcing his head down and hands deep into his pockets he picked up the pace. He couldn't help but fiddle with the stone for support.

'Hey hold up,' Graham called to William, who was now five or six paces ahead. 'Want to walk to school with us?'

William couldn't believe his ears, this really was getting too much. It was like he was now living in a parallel universe. With a huge smile on his face, the words 'yes please' caught in his throat as he spotted Iris leaving the sweet shop. 'M-m-maybe next time,' he finally managed, in what he hoped was his cool voice. 'I'm meeting a friend today, catch up with you guys later though, yeah?'

'For sure, laters William!' Graham smiled as he ran off to high five each of the four lads waiting for him.

'Wanna try a Super Sour Saturn Zinger? They're new today!' Iris asked once the group of boys had gone. She didn't wait for an answer, instead just popped a sugary sphere straight into his mouth.

It was strange seeing her out of uniform, probably because he'd only been friends with her for one day and so that was how he was used to seeing her. But she looked exactly as he imagined she would in her own clothes as they suited her personality to a T; turquoise glitter wellies, yellow and purple spotty tights, a dark purple corduroy dungaree dress, a mustard colour, long sleeve polo neck top, the thickest blue duffle coat he'd ever seen, a black woolly scarf with bright green aliens on it and a narwhal bobble hat. William thought she looked simply amazing.

'Wow they ARE super sour!' His face twisting this way and that as the zingy flavour made his cheeks pull together. 'Lemon?'

'Close! Yuzu, they're from Japan,' she smiled brightly, twiddling another sugary globe between her finger and thumb. 'You look different in your normal clothes,' she added between chews, looking him up and down as if realising he was out of uniform for the first time.

William couldn't help but notice that she sounded unimpressed, he fiddled with his stone as he began to feel insecure about his new look. As if sensing his concern Iris quickly added, 'you don't look bad or anything, it's just I imagined you'd look different to the other boys at school that's all, but this,' she waved a hand, indicating his expensive ensemble of black, white and blue sports-wear, 'this is nice too. I really like your scarf though.'

William almost blushed, and instinctively felt for the tatty wool, its softness bringing a smile to his face, 'thanks, it's my dad's.'

As they walked through the familiar streets, over the field, past the park and onto Middletown's high street, Iris chatted excitedly about the boss she was trying to beat on Captain Bubblegum 2, even though William had never played a video game in his life he eagerly hung on to her every word.

'I'm on level 21 now, the boss is called Dracola,' she explained sucking on one of the Birthday Mallow Squeaks William had offered her. He had decided to make the packet last for as long as possible by only having a couple a day, but was more than happy to share that ration with Iris. 'He uses a weaponised soda bottle to keep you from reaching the keys you need in order to escape. I must have played it like 18 times last night but I still can't figure out how it's done. Every time I get close, BOOM, covered in soda, game over. I think I may have to...'

William gently touched Iris' arm and nodded towards the bank where two large men were acting strangely. They were seemingly taking it in turns to walk past the bank's door, look inside then go back to their car, where they talked to one another for a few seconds, and then the whole thing started all over again. Something didn't feel right. He reached for the stone, and waited for it to warm in his palm.

'Iris, you go on, I'm just going to check something out.'

'Wait, what? Where?'

'Over there, by the bench or go ahead on to school. I'm sure it's nothing. I'll meet you there in a bit.'

'Yeah right matey, we're partners now. Whatever you're up to, I want in.'

William studied her face, she looked serious, like when mum tells Brian; 'No more biscuits! No I actually mean it this time. No really. No, not one more, no more! The whole packet is gone. There are no more biscuits Brian!'

'Okay,' William finally agreed, 'but stay back and act casual.'

'Roger that,' Iris saluted and winked at the same time, then after taking a look around walked a few feet away and leaned against a tree. She took out her yoyo and began performing a variety of tricks with it, which although were very impressive, wasn't exactly what William had had in mind when he told her to 'act casual'.

'What are you doing?' William asked.

'Just taking it easy Wills, you know being chill and all that,' Iris said strangely, which William supposed was her 'acting casual' voice.

'Right, well, good. You stay here, I'm going over there to get a closer look. Be right back,' he gave her a nod then crossed the road at the traffic lights, all the while keeping his eyes fixed on the two odd men. Both were rather burly looking, and if they were animals, they would definitely have been rhinos; short but stocky, with chunky arms and legs, no neck, just big bowling balls for heads. They were very similar looking, so much so he decided they were probably brothers; neither had hair, just big bushy brown eyebrows, narrow hawk-like eyes and bulbous noses. One of them was whispering in the other one's ear, while the other listened with a grimacing expression on his face, all the while thumping a clenched fist into his palm, it reminded William of something he'd seen before. Of course! Maddox! Could it be? Was that Maddox's dad and uncle? There was certainly a gorilla-like family resemblance. Now William was just metres from them and the bank. He gripped the stone hard as he wondered what to do next.

'Ah, so it's these two you've got your eye on, eh?' Iris said, making him jump.

'Iris, you have got to stop doing that!' He gripped his chest, trying to slow his racing heart. 'You're going to give me a heart attack!'

'No can do William, I'm part ninja, part pirate, part intergalactic space warrior... didn't I tell you that when we first met?'

William shook his head, busy forcing his now ragged breathing to slow down.

Iris shrugged, 'oh well, you know now. So what's the plan?' she asked, bobbing and weaving a barrage of invisible punches.

'Well first we need to play it cool,' he managed, trying to restrain her flailing limbs, 'I think those guys are up to something.'

Just then a flurry of snowflakes began sprinkling themselves all over the little village green and the rooftops of the shops that encircled it. As a customer left the bank, the door stayed open just long enough for a wave of warm air to rush out and almost grab them. Inside William spotted Cafe Lady. 'Come on,' he said, 'I think we should tell someone.'

Cafe Lady looked both surprised and pleased to see William again, and was equally excited to meet Iris, whom William had talked at great lengths about. Cafe Lady explained she was just about to deposit this week's takings, which had been down due to the bad weather. 'Oh, but you must pop in again William,' she smiled, touching him gently on the arm. 'It was so lovely talking to you, and Iris you must come too. Perhaps later after school? Speaking of which, shouldn't you two be there now?'

William looked at his watch, she was right, 'we just had to tell someone first that there are two men outside the bank acting, well, a bit weird.'

'Oh dear, weird? In what way?'

'Well,' William began, but was abruptly interrupted as the two men, now with masks on; one a lion, the other a baby, charged into the bank.

'EVERYONE GET DOWN ON THE FLOOR!' the lion roared, waving a gun in the air.

CHAPTER 8

The Robbery

William froze, as you probably would have done if shouted at by two terrifying bank robbers. It was only when Iris tugged on William's trouser leg that he suddenly realised the importance of joining her on the bank's shiny granite floor.

'Just stay calm,' Cafe Lady whispered to them, but while her tone was soothing her eyes gave away her worry.

Meanwhile the lion-faced robber was yelling at the bank teller, demanding she fill their suitcases with cash, and lots of it.

'We have to do something!' Iris whispered to William, her voice tinged with panic.

William stared at her agog, first Maddox and now these two, he couldn't help but wonder if Iris had a death wish or maybe she had a secret superpower like invincibility he didn't know about. 'What can we do?' He asked, completely puzzled.

'We have to stop them!'

'I don't know Iris, they've got guns!'

'But look! See that little old lady over there?' Iris nodded towards a little old lady who had refused to "get down on the floor", no bigger than a seven-year-old, she was bundled up in so many layers of knitted clothing that she looked almost like a ball of wool herself. The baby-faced robber stuck his tongue out in concentration as he tried to prise the large glass jar of cash she held gripped in her mitten-covered hands. The old lady wasn't given up that easily, vigorously shaking her head and holding the jar tighter still.

'That's Old Mrs Hobbs!' Iris implored, as though William ought to know who she was, but he just pulled a *"I have no idea who that is"* kind of face. 'She has that pet charity, you know "Hobbs' Home for Homeless pets"?'

'Oh I know!' William smiled, 'she took in Nibbler, after mum said Kevin couldn't be trusted with him anymore.'

'Well then, you know how important that donation money is, and we CAN'T let them take it!'

'Quiet over there!' The lion-masked thug growled at Iris from where he stood waiting impatiently at the counter, as the young lady filling his bags with bundles of bank notes from the vault, shook with fear and tears. 'Stop your blubbering!' He thundered at her. 'And what's going on over there?' He waved his gun at Old Mrs

Hobbs.

'She won't 'and it over bruv!' The robber wearing the baby mask wailed.

'Then make her! And don't call me bruv!' He added with a menacing hiss.

'Sorry bruv, I mean Rory,' the baby-faced robber giggled. 'Get it? Roar-y, Rory? You know, cos lion's go "roar" don't they. Clever innit? That was his idea,' he told Old Mrs Hobbs who held her money as close to her as if it were one of her pets. 'But that's not his real name, his real name is...'

'Dimples!' Rory the Robber yelled. 'Are you really that stupid? Now hurry up and nab the loot off all these saps. Now!'

'Sorry bruv - I mean Rory,' simpered Dimples, and with that he whipped the donations out of Old Mrs Hobbs' arms as though it were candy from a baby, then proceeded to point his gun at the next bank customer; a young man in a very smart suit. 'Hand over your wallet, phone and other valuables, please and fank you.'

'William!' Iris whispered, 'we have to act now. He'll come to us in a minute and take whatever we have.'

'Oh no!' Cafe Lady realised in alarm. 'This is all the money I made this week, which is barely anything. How will I tell Peter he can't have that new Bubblegum game he wanted?'

'You're a great mum,' William suddenly found himself saying. 'You don't need to buy Peter all the best stuff. I'm sure he'll understand if money is tight. He has you and that's all he really needs.'

Cafe Lady's eyes immediately glistened with tears, 'thank you for saying that William, I think I've been waiting for someone to tell me that for years. Before Pete's dad left we used to be able to afford all the best things money could buy, but that all changed when we divorced and since then I've been trying my hardest to keep things normal for him, but times are hard and I find myself going without so he can have more. But you're right, things have to change. I have to tell him the truth. If we ever get out of here.'

'We will,' Iris took Cafe Lady's hand in hers, and the woman let out a loud sob, which inadvertently drew the attention of the baby-faced thug.

'Stop your boo-hooing lady and hand over the dough.'

Threatened with the gun, Cafe Lady had no choice but to do as the robber asked, who snatched the takings away with a rather insincere 'fank you', then stomped over to an elderly man who was attempting to hide behind a rather tall, but altogether too thin fake plant, and because he was quivering so much, made its plastic leaves jiggle and wiggle as though it was giggling.

With the enormous robber's back turned, Iris rolled her eyes emphatically at William and said, 'he'll be coming for us next! I don't know about you but I don't want him checking my bag. I brought my new video game on the portable console so we could play it on the walk home after school. I've got all the way to level 21 so he's definitely not having that! I'm not starting all over again. You must have things you don't want to lose too William?'

Now you might think William's first thought would be the magic stone in his pocket, surely a priceless piece of treasure in anyone's opinion, but instead his hand shot up to his neck where his fingers felt for that tatty red scarf.

'I have an idea,' whispered William.

CHAPTER 9

Quick thinking

Within ten minutes of the robbers entering the bank, they had successfully filled two huge suitcases with cash that the cashier had been forced to hand over, and stuffed another holdall full of valuables and money that Dimples had wrestled from the hostages.

'What about these two?' the baby-faced robber shouted over to his brother who was now busy nicking the bank's pens, wedging them into every pocket of his long grey coat.

'What about them?'

'Well, they're kids.'

'And?'

'But they're about the same as little Maddo…'

'Dimples!' Rory almost screamed marching towards his brother aggressively, his hard-heeled shoes smacking loudly against the shiny floor, 'what did I say about using our real names!?'

'You said not to use them, but does that include your boy's name too?'

'Of course it does, you bum dummy!' And with that Rory whacked Dimples on the head.

'Ow!' Dimples cried, 'that really hurt! And what's a bum dummy?'

'I dunno, Maddox says it. Wait, are you crying?'

'No,' muttered Dimples quietly, but clearly he was because his whole body began to quake as he let out little sobs. 'It's just not very nice when you call me mean names like bum dummy, nozzle brain and snot crumpet.'

'Oh pull yourself together, we haven't got time for this. Let's just go before the cops show up.' Rory grabbed his brother's arm roughly and pulled him and the suitcases towards the door.

It was now or never thought William gripping the stone tightly, it was so hot it felt like it might burn a hole in his hand.

'I can't believe you're leaving already,' William managed, stutter-free, in a loud and clear voice that echoed off the bank's walls.

The criminals froze, then slowly turned around and saw William getting to his feet.

'What did you say?' snarled Rory, striding back to William.

'William, no! Lie down and stay quiet,' Cafe Lady implored him from the floor.

'I said...' William held his nerve, casually brushing the dust off his new clothes with his free hand. 'I can't believe you're leaving with just that,' he gestured to their luggage as though they were tea bags rather than bags loaded with cash.

Rory let a 'pah' as though William were mad, which Dimples copied, but clearly confused by the exchange added, 'hold up, what do ya mean?'

'All I'm saying,' William added coolly. 'Is you've obviously forgotten about the vault of priceless artefacts. You know? All the fancy stuff rich people and places like auction houses, museums, and palaces store here for safe keeping.'

William squeezed his stone and wished for his plan to work, as the thugs looked at each other and then back at William, trying to decide whether he was telling the truth.

'Are you seriously telling me you did all this,' William waved his arms towards the hostages still lying on the ground, 'for a couple of bags of cash? Wow! Okay then.'

'What? No! Wait, yes,' Dimples scratched his head and shifted his weight as he thought about what William had said. 'Bruv- I mean Rory, did we? I'm confused.'

'Of course we knew,' Rory said proudly, his head turning this way and that, clearly looking for the secret vault. 'It has all that, um that, um expensive stuff in it, like um…'

'Priceless jewellery, bars of gold, one-of-a-kind antiques…' William added helpfully.

'Yeah like I said, expensive stuff.'

'I read in the paper that the Queen's bracelet was even being held here at the moment,' William offered, thinking on his feet. 'You know the one with all those diamonds and rubies?'

Folding his arms Rory grimaced, 'of course I know that! I know lots of fings!' But the flash of uncertainty that flickered in his dark eyes beneath the mask, gave away his true thoughts.

'Did you!? I didn't,' pouted Dimples with a shrug, 'I didn't even know you read the newspaper.'

'Of course I do! Usually when it's the wrapping for my Fish and Chips but I still do, anyway enough of that. Where's this vault then?' He stormed over to the bank teller, waving his gun in her face, closer this time. Overcome with the drama of it all she fainted dramatically, falling bottom first onto a comfy leather seat behind the desk. 'For Pete's Sake! You! Fact Boy!'

'Me?' William asked innocently.

'Yeah you! Tell me where this secret vault is then or I'm going to start shooting!' Rory's temper was starting to get the better of him which is exactly what William had hoped for. He knew that when people got mad it made their decision making worse. He knew this after extensive months of watching baby Brian attempt to fit shapes into a shape sorter. Every time without fail, he'd get stuck on the diamond one, thinking it was a square, the angrier he got the worse he was at fitting the rest of the shapes in until finally he'd throw the whole thing across the room. Once he even knocked Kevin's goldfish bowl clean off the side table. The fish died, so his mum replaced it with a frozen chicken nugget. To this day Kevin's still unaware his beloved fish "Tiddler" is a chunk of poultry covered in breadcrumbs.

'Isn't it obvious?' William laughed. 'Think about it. If you wanted to hide something, where's the best place to do it?'

'In a bank?' Dimples answered at the top of his voice, thinking he had the answer right and as such was clearly very proud of himself.

'Underground!' Rory said knowingly, then punched the air as if he'd just won a competition.

'In a teapot?' Old Mrs Hobbs chimed in, not really sure what was going on.

'No, no, and definitely no,' William answered coolly, pacing over to a door on the other side of the bank. 'Everyone knows the best place to hide something is in…' He whipped open the door to reveal a well-stocked cleaning cupboard, a waft of disinfectant swarming out as he held it open for the bank robbers to get a good look inside.

'In a broom cupboard?!' Dimples said, utterly confused.

'No… ' William answered, a smile creeping over his face, '…in plain sight.'

CHAPTER 10

Fool me once

'You what?' Thundered Rory, unable to believe what William was saying was true. 'You expect me to believe that the Queen stashes her jewels in this, what? Janitor's closet?'

'That's right,' William smiled. 'Who on earth would think of looking amongst stacks of toilet roll, or bottles of floor cleaner for bars of gold or priceless diamond necklaces? No one! Ingenious isn't it?! In fact, I heard from my friend, Graham, um, er, Truewis, whose dad works for the bank, that those brooms aren't actually brooms at all, oh no. If you pull on that one right at the back it opens a secret door behind those shelves that leads down to where all the ultra, high-end, super duper expensive treasure is kept.'

The ten seconds or so Rory weighed all this up in his mind felt like forever to William. His palms were so sweaty now he was terrified he might drop the magic stone, which was hidden in his clenched fist. 'Still don't believe me? Okay, let me show you then.' William stepped over a mop bucket, and moved past several stacks of sponges until he was finally concealed out of sight behind a hat stand completely covered in cleaners' uniforms. 'A ha!' He shouted moments later as he returned back into the bank foyer where the hostages, as well as the robbers were eagerly waiting to see what William had found.

A resounding chorus of 'oohs' and 'aahhs' burst from the captives' mouths, who were either really impressed or just sneakily playing along, but either way, it was the response William had hoped for when he held his purple stone up in the air. Urged into action by the hostages' enthusiasm, Rory snatched the stone and held it aloft under the bright light of the bank's central chandelier where it twinkled magnificently.

'What is it?' gasped Dimples.

'Don't you know?' Remarked William all aloof.

'Yeah, don't you know?' Rory joined in on making Dimples feel foolish, but clearly none the wiser himself. 'But, er, yeah you tell him what it is, kid.'

'That is the Amazonian Amethyst, the largest of its kind to be found this side of 1982. I heard the rumour that it was being stored here for the Prince of Monaco, but I didn't think it was actually true.'

'Bruv there could be loads more stuff like that in there!' Dimples said, bouncing from foot to foot with glee. 'The kid found that one so fast! Just imagine what else is in there and bruv just fink what must be down in that vault!'

Rory twirled the gem in his fingers, looking at it this way and that in the light. William's whole body felt like it was made of jelly. After what felt like an eternity Rory finally turned to his brother and said, 'empty the bags.'

'What? All of them?' Dimples asked dumbfounded.

'That's what I said, didn't I? Forget the money! We'll get loads more for all the jewels and gold stashed in there and we need these bags to carry everything. Now hurry up!' Rory growled, slipping William's stone into his pocket. With that, the brothers unzipped their luggage and turned all the bank's money and customer's possessions onto the floor.

'Now you,' Rory pointed his gun at William, 'get in there and open the vault door.'

Now any other person may have begun to panic in this situation, but William had already realised that the robbers might ask him to do this, so answering very calmly and very matter of factly he said, 'sure, but I should warn you that this door,' he pointed to a grey cleaning cupboard door, 'will automatically close and lock before the secret door opens. It's a high-tech safety feature that all the best banks have, and well, you know the saying, "finders keepers" and all that?'

'Hey wait!' Dimples shouted. 'No fair! He's going to get all our loot!'

'Not if I have anything to do with it,' Rory said, pushing William out of the way and climbing past the buckets, collection of mops and boxes of rubber gloves. 'Grab those bags and get in here Dimples.'

Dimples did as his brother demanded and closed the door behind him. The moment he did William took off his scarf and looped it through the door's handle, tying it tightly to the fire extinguisher attached on the wall next to the cupboard. 'Quick!' he pleaded to the captives, 'someone call the police!'

The customers scrambled to their feet and dove onto the pile of valuables, searching for their own phones and dialling 999 to report the robbery.

'That. Was. Amazing!' Iris' eyes twinkled with pride as she grabbed William and gave his whole body a huge squeeze. 'You're a hero William! How did you come up with such a great plan? I can't believe those two ninny pants fell for it!'

But before William could reply, there was an almighty BANG on the other side of the broom cupboard door, then another which was even louder than the first, and then another which was followed up by an enormous kick that took the door clean off its hinges. Out stepped the two burly brothers, their bodies hunched aggressively like a pair of steaming mad bulls who had just seen red.

'YOU THINK YOU'RE SO CLEVER DON'T YOU KID?!' Rory yelled so loudly it made the chandelier on the ceiling twirl and tinkle as the glass ornaments danced into one another. He thundered towards William, bearing down on him like an angry grizzly bear. William protectively used his body to block Iris, but within a few steps they were both backed into a corner. 'Suppose you thought it would be funny, eh? Making us look like a couple of nitwits! Well I'll show you who's the fool!'

'Yeah! And you made me get all wet!' Dimples interrupted with a pitiful moan, pointing to the lower half of his trouser leg. 'It was all dark and scary in there with the door shut and I put my foot straight into a bucket of dirty water! And we never did find the right broomstick to open the vault either did we bruv?'

'There was no broomstick lever you brainless bum biscuit!' The thug turned on his brother, bashing him on the head again.

'Ow!' He cried, rubbing the red lump as it appeared on his bald dome. 'Yes there were, I found loads! I just couldn't see which was the right one to open the secret door.'

'There is no secret vault! It was a trick! He tricked us!'

'Oh! Well then. That wasn't very nice was it?' Dimples pouted, genuinely upset. 'But wait, what about that shiny purple one? We still have that! That's gotta be worth summit hasn't it?'

The lion-faced robber slapped his palm onto his mask in exasperation, 'you are such a nincompoop! This!' he shouted, holding William's stone aloft, 'is clearly a fake!' And with that he launched it across the foyer, in the direction of the hostages.

'Now I'm going to teach YOU a lesson clever clogs!' Rory leaned over William like a huge troll with really stinky breath and even worse body odour, his fist raised high, ready to strike.

William closed his eyes and braced himself, but as he lent back slightly his face brushed against Iris's as she was still stood behind him. They were so close he could smell the sweet, zingy scent of yuzu still on her breath. *That's it!* he thought, an idea jumping into his head.

'Wait!' he yelled, causing Rory to pause his strike mid air. 'How about one of these instead?' William showed the criminals his bag of Birthday Cake Mallowsqueaks.

The bulky brothers peered in the bag and then at each other.

'Sweets?' Rory scoffed, seemingly unimpressed.

'Sweets! Ooh don't mind if I do!' Dimples said politely, leaning forward to take one daintily with his chubby fingers, but just as his hand moved within centimetres of the paper bag, William threw it up in the air. The marble-like balls rained down across the smooth granite floor, scattering all around the robbers' feet. While the rhino-like men took a few seconds to work out what had happened, Iris did the same with her Super Sour Saturn Zingers; the little hard-shelled spheres pinging here, there and everywhere like a shower of pinballs. All that was left to do was to give the robbers a little nudge, which Iris provided courtesy of a mightily impressive karate chop to Rory's gut, who then fell like a domino into his brother.

Much to his own surprise, Dimples actually caught Rory, but immediately the hard balls found their way under the men's big feet, causing them to slip and slide all over the floor, as though they were performing a choreographed skating routine on ice, until eventually they crashed spectacularly into one another and Dimples landed splat on top of his brother. With the marble sweets still underneath them, the pair skidded on Rory's stomach right across the bank's foyer, as though he was a human sleigh.

'Wheeee!' Dimples cried excitedly.

Cafe Lady carefully got to her feet and swiftly pulled open the bank's door to allow the skidding duo to shoot outside, across what was now a very icy path, and plough head first into a dog poo bin. Which, not having been emptied for some days, was stacked dangerously high with a mound of multi-coloured plastic bags, all of which then fell on top of the robbers in a succession of little splats. What was worse for the thugs was that not all the bags had been tied up properly.

William's hands trembled with adrenaline as he scooped up his scarf, and while gracefully dodging the treacherous terrain of scattered sweets, made his way outside where the snow had really started to come down.

'Quick, give me a hand,' William urged Cafe Lady and Iris, who helped him tie the unconscious men together with the scarf.

Snoring in unison as loudly as a pair of baby hippos, their enormously round bellies grew with each deep breath. Now pulled very tight, William's scarf, which was already rather tatty, started to unravel.

'Need a hand?' Old Lady Hobbs called softly as she shuffled slowly out of the bank, taking careful, tiny mouse-like steps on the slippy pavement. Once she'd joined the trio she began removing her many scarves, which amounted to five in total. Next she handed them to William who with Cafe Lady's help made a rope that was more than long enough to hold the burly men, who were still deep in slumber, snoring as contentedly as though they were safe and warm in their beds, not tied to a stinky dog waste bin with scatterings of poop and snow on their bald heads.

A cold wind whipped around them, causing Old Mrs Hobbs, who now looked very small and slight indeed, to bristle uncontrollably as the gust played with the fine hairs on her head. William shrugged off his sports jacket and hung it round the elderly woman's shoulders to keep her warm.

Her smile made her face crinkle so tightly William could barely see her eyes, 'thank you,' she said, hugging him around the waist, 'for everything'.

When she finally let him go she placed something in his hand. It was his stone, cracked into two pieces.

The wail of five police cars, two ambulances and a fire engine speeding onto the high street drowned out the sound of the small sob that escaped William's lips.

CHAPTER 11

The reward

The week that followed the attempted bank robbery had been nothing short of craziness!

When the police arrived and heard what had happened, word soon got around and William, Iris, Old Lady Hobbs and Cafe Lady (or Mrs Potts, as it turned out was her actual name) became overnight celebrities.

For William things felt very strange, because in just a few days he'd gone from feeling as though he was completely invisible to becoming a hometown hero.

That evening, just a few hours after the Bullburn brothers' failed robbery, William and the others appeared on the local TV news. His whole family gathered around their television in the front room, all agog. They just couldn't believe this was their William being interviewed by the news reporter, who in William's opinion made the whole thing seem much more dramatic and dangerous than it actually was.

Headmaster Creedicorn had held a special assembly the following day, all about how to be a good citizen and had William and Iris come and stand right in front of the whole school to retell the story, which Iris greatly embellished with details William knew not to be true. For instance, according to Iris's version of events at one point William had leapt up into the air, swung on the bank's chandelier, back-flipped and karate kicked the "eight-foot-tall" burglars in the gut, sending them skidding across the sweet laden floor at 100 mph!

William had also appeared in the local newspaper not once, but twice. The first was for the bank robbery, while the second was when he collected a special bravery award from the bank. As well as getting a fancy-framed certificate he was also given a ridiculously oversized cheque for an awful lot of money, more money than his family had had in their whole lives. In fact his mum had cried when William had told her he wanted her to have it all the following day, which was a Saturday, and boy was William glad! No school kids chanting his name as he entered the gates, no journalists pushing microphones under his nose asking for his opinion on this or that, and he'd even started to avoid the shops because the shopkeepers kept making such a big fuss of him whenever he went past one of them; giving him bags of free stuff and patting him on the head like a puppy that had performed a trick. At first it was kind of nice, but now their tiny house was filled with the most random things and he was sure he was losing hair from all the rubbing people were doing to his head. Just from where William was sitting at the kitchen table he could see the fishing rod from the angling shop, the 16-piece plier set from the hardware store, and the 17th-century Bavarian Cuckoo Clock from the Antiques place, which were all waiting to be put away. He found it hard to believe, but he was suddenly missing feeling invisible.

'I can't accept this William, it's yours, you deserve it for what you and your friends did, maybe you should share it with them?' William's mother managed, feeling for the chair next to her son, because she couldn't tear her eyes away from all the zeros on the cheque.

'But they got a reward too, remember?' William explained, holding his face in his hands as though the weight of the world were on his shoulders. 'Iris says she's going to invest hers in a video game company she likes, Mrs Hobbs is going to use hers to open more homes for more homeless animals, and Cafe Lady, I mean Mrs Potts, is going to refurbish The Chipped Teapot Cafe to make it look all fancy and new. I don't need anything mum, I want you to have it. Maybe we could get a bigger house?' He smiled gently, not wanting to cause any offence to his hard-working mum, but with so many of them in so few bedrooms, surely a little more space would be nice for everyone. 'Besides, I don't deserve it.'

All William's mum could do was stare at her son dumbfounded. 'Not deserve it?!' she eventually managed. 'My darling boy, nothing could be further from the truth. What you did saved more than just money. People could have got really hurt or worse, and because of your quick thinking and bravery that didn't happen. Thanks to you, two of the naughtiest men in Middletown are behind bars, and will stay that way for a very long time. William my love, you ARE a hero.'

'I'm not,' he said staring at the table, suddenly embarrassed, tears forming in his eyes. 'I wish everyone would stop calling me that. I'm a phoney!'

'William what are you saying? You're not making any sense!'

'It wasn't me who did all those things, it was, it was…' he took a deep breath, ready to finally admit the truth to the world, 'it was the stone.'

'The stone? What stone? William, I don't understand.'

'This stone,' he said almost angrily, as he took the broken shards of gemstone from his pocket and placed them in front of her, 'it gave me the power to do what I did. It's been granting everything I've wished for. That stone is the real hero, not me.'

William looked at his mum, who looked at him in utter confusion, and then at the pieces of gemstone, and then back at him again. 'William darling, I'm going to need a little more information sweetie. Why do you think this stone gave you, what was it? Special powers?'

Taking a deep breath William told her the whole story; everything from getting the parcel from Grandpa Rupert, to Kevin getting in the bin, to her giving them ice cream for dinner, Mr Fizzy giving him and Iris free sweets, avoiding detention with Mr Creedicorn, miraculously stopping Maddox's attack, Cafe Lady giving him all those cakes and cool clothes, and every single part of his so-called "act of bravery" at the bank. After he was finished with his long tale he slumped forward on his arms and moaned, 'see, it wasn't me, none of it, it was the stone. It made all of those incredible things happen, and it helped me to feel incredible. But not anymore, I bet it won't work now it's broken.'

After taking a minute or so to process all the information she'd heard, William's mum picked up the purple gem and looked at it closely. 'William I'm going to tell you something and I'm not sure if it's the right or wrong thing to say, but I have to go with what my mummy instincts are telling me right this second.'

William lifted his head and wiped his cheeks free of tears. Was she going to say he was unwell and have him see a doctor, was she going to say he should give the money back to the bank, which was probably the right thing to do, or would she be angry that he'd lied all this time? After taking a big deep breath he was ready to hear her verdict.

'William. This stone is not magic.'

'But…'

'William listen to me, please,' she soothed, gently touching his hand with hers. 'The reason most of those things happened my love wasn't because of magic, it was because of you. William, before last week, before you got this stone, you hadn't spoken a single word for over a year. Not since your dad passed away.'

William instinctively reached up to his neck, needing to feel the comfort and sense of security his dad's old scarf gave him. Anxiously he turned his head quickly towards the front door where he saw it safely hung up with the coats. A loud sigh of relief passed his lips. It was more than just a scarf to him. It was the big beaming smile his dad would give everyone as he wrapped the scarf around his neck before setting off to work. It was all the winters he and his dad would use the scarf to dress the snowmen they'd make year after year. It was his dad hugging him close the moment he got home, the soft wool tickling his cheek as he held him tight. It even used to smell of his dad, but somewhere during the time he'd been gone, the scent had faded away.

Back at the bank, it was the scarf he feared losing more than anything. That was his "valuable" item. Not a watch, phone or games console, and it was the fear of the robbers taking it away from him that spurred him into action. The thought of losing a tatty old red scarf that no one would look twice at. But to him, that scarf was everything.

'William, when you spoke to Kevin that day, it meant everything to him. He would have done anything you asked. It was like you came back to life right in front of him, me too! When you asked for ice cream, I would have given you all the ice cream in Middletown if I could have. Just to hear your precious little voice again, it was everything. You were always a quiet boy, never one to make a fuss, but when your dad passed away, it was like a piece of you went with him.' Tears began rolling down her face one after another. Quickly brushing them away she added, 'what else? Yes, okay so I don't have an answer as to why Cafe Lady, I mean Mrs Potts, gave you all those things, other than she is a very nice person and probably just realised what a lovely, polite and wonderful boy you are and was more than happy to. So that's that, and oh Mr. Fizzy, well that's an easy one; he's Iris' grandfather.'

William's mouth fell open. How could he have missed that?! Thinking back to the day he first met Iris, it was in Mr. Fizzy's shop, the old man had even given her a wink. No wonder she always had a fresh bag of sweets every morning. William smiled, the obviousness of it all dawning on him.

'As for what happened to Maddox,' his mum continued. 'I'm just as clueless as you are, but I will say that I am happy he is no longer at your school.'

William sniffed and managed a smile. He felt bad for Maddox, having his dad and uncle taken to prison wasn't nice at all, but knowing the school bully had moved with his mum to a town far, far away was a big relief, especially as being his father's vanquisher would have put a huge target on his back.

'But what about what happened at the bank?'

'William, that was all you,' his mum smiled, squeezing his hand. 'It was your bravery, quick thinking and cleverness that saved the day. Not this,' she waved the bits of stone in the air. 'I'm sure if we look close enough it probably says "Made in Germany" somewhere. After all, your Grandpa Rupert never was one to rely on.'

William was confused. Could she really be right? It did all make sense what she was saying if he really thought about it. When William's dad had passed away it felt as though a big hole had opened up inside of him and sucked out all the happiness from his body. He had felt as though he'd never be able to smile or laugh ever again, and any confidence or sense of self that he did have, shrivelled up and withered away. Then he just stopped talking. At first it was because he just didn't feel like he had anything to say, but the longer it lasted the more he withdrew from life, fading a little more every day without even realising it, until days rolled into weeks and the weeks into months, and eventually everyone around him, quite unintentionally, stopped noticing him.

'Still don't believe me?' She asked.

William shrugged, he wasn't sure what to think. He'd liked thinking he had magic powers, but maybe this was better somehow, knowing the magic came from inside him instead.

'Okay then,' she said, straightening up, 'ask me for anything, anything you want. Whatever you want more than anything in the world and see what I say.'

William thought for a moment, then a big smile exploded across his face. He knew exactly what he wanted and immediately reached for the segments of stone, but his mum was faster and moved them out of reach.

'Not with the stone,' she smiled.

Taking a deep breath William closed his eyes and said all in one go, 'please can I have a friend over after school to stay for dinner, but not one of your surprise dinners which are nice but a, well, a normal dinner, like other kids have, like chicken nuggets, chips and beans, with ice cream, but for pudding, not on top of the beans?'

William could feel his heart beating. This was it; the moment of truth.

A smile unfurled across William's mum's face, 'well it's funny you should say that because...'

Just then there was a loud knock at the front door. For a minute William was sure it was Mrs Patel returning Kevin from her property again, but as soon as he heard the voice of the person entering his home he leapt out of his seat and ran to greet them.

'Iris!' He almost sang and gave her a cuddle so tight it made her sneeze and giggle all at the same time.

EPILOGUE

The Truth

It took a while for things to settle down in Middletown; the would-have-been-bank-robbery was the most exciting thing ever to have happened in the small town, and even months later people were still cheering William as he walked into school, down the street, or in a shop. He'd got used to the attention, but had decided to start wearing gel in his hair to put off the would-be-head-patters.

And it wasn't just William who was feeling the aftershocks of fame. Thanks to all the publicity they had received, Mrs Hobbs' Home for Homeless Pets in Uppertown, Middletown and Lower-town had all become so well known that every single one of the unwanted pets she once sheltered had been lovingly adopted, including a new fish for Kevin, and twin hamsters for Faye and May. As such Mrs. Hobbs was currently taking a well-earned holiday in the Bahamas with her 21-year-old boyfriend Brad.

Similarly, Mrs Potts' Chipped Tea Pot Cafe was doing a booming trade since she had it redecorated, her customers eager to hear the tale of 'The Great Bungled Bank Robbery' with a cup of tea and slice of homemade cake. Peter, who after a heart to heart with his mother, came to understand the importance of giving more and demanding less, which is why he now helps out in the cafe after school and on weekends, and has become firm friends with William who got a Saturday job there.

As for Iris, she was still her wonderful bubbly self, only with a gaming empire at her fingertips. Since receiving her award and investing it in several video game startups, Iris helped create the concepts for five new games, all due for release next Christmas. Between school and overseeing her business portfolio Iris was a lot busier than before, but she still had time for her best friend, who despite becoming an overnight celebrity and moving into a much bigger house in a nicer part of town, was still the same old William. In fact just as he had got used to feeling invisible once upon a time, now he'd got used to being noticed and it wasn't all bad. He was doing great in school, academically and socially; he had better grades and more friends than he could ever remember having before, and things were certainly a lot easier for everyone at his school now that Maddox Bullburn had left.

But it was that so-called 'fight' with Maddox that had played on William's mind for the longest time. He could understand what his mum had said about the transformation in his character and the generosity of others to explain why things changed so dramatically for him that day, but the one thing he couldn't work out was how he defeated Maddox.

He hadn't used the stone for months now, not since that day it broke at the bank, but he wanted to know what had happened, it was the final mystery in this crazy puzzle he had lived through. So one particularly bright and sunny early Spring morning William finally summoned the courage to reveal everything to Iris in the hope that she might have an answer.

'So you thought a gemstone your grandpa had posted to you from deep within a South American rainforest was magic and it made all the things you wished for come true?' Iris managed between chomps of the new sweets her grandfather had just popped on the shelves that very morning; *Exasperatingly Chewy Chunky Monkeys.*

Now Iris had said it out loud he knew it was bonkers. He buried his face down inside the comfort of his scarf as if to hide, 'I know, it's ridiculous, I'm ridiculous.'

'Not at all,' she said, finally finishing her mouthful. 'Well ridiculous in a good way maybe, but I can see why you thought that, and if it meant that me and you became friends because of it, well then it was magic wasn't it. Magic, because it was the best thing that ever happened to me.'

Her smile made William's heart feel eight times bigger. Bringing his head out of his scarf like a tortoise emerging from its shell he asked, 'so then? What do you think really happened to Maddox? Who or what hurt him that day?'

After casually popping a sweet in William's mouth, Iris threw another in the air, expertly catching it in her own. Then casually mid-chew, she pulled out the yoyo she always kept in her pocket, and with mind-boggling speed and force unleashed it dead ahead, like a whip cracking or lightning striking, and then in a blink of an eye the yoyo was back in her hand. 'Oh William, don't you know?' she smiled knowingly, 'a magician never reveals her secrets.'

❊ ❊ ❊

'Oh is that you William?' His mother called cheerily from the kitchen later that day when he returned home.

'Oh hi mum!' He gave her a quick kiss on the cheek as he entered the huge kitchen, which was bigger than the entirety of their old house, 'oh bonjour also Monsieur Leclerc, so what's for dinner tonight?'

'Your favourite William, as requested!' The live-in chef said excitedly, in his deep, rich French accent, 'pépites de poulet, frites et fèves au lard.'

'Yes! Chicken nuggets, chips and beans!' William was so happy he punched the air, delighted that "Surprise nights" were now a thing of the past, thanks to the professional chef they gladly paid to cook their meals.

'William this came for you today,' his mother said, handing him a brown paper parcel.

Taking it up to his extremely large bedroom, complete with video game area, vending machine, giant gumball picker, and a bunk bed which instead of having a ladder, featured a curly slide and rope net. Thankfully all the Wallberson children now had their own rooms, so William no longer had to share with his brother Kevin, who had grown out of his 'being-an-emergency-vehicle-phase' and now believed himself to be a chicken called Barry Fatfeathers.

William tore open the brown paper parcel on his bed, where out fell a letter and a stone of emerald green. Scanning the letter from Grandpa Rupert, William's heart leapt into his mouth when he read the words, 'this stone, from the heart of the Peruvian jungle, is said to have once belonged to the infamous Shai-Tu-Kamen. It's said to gift the owner the power of invisibility, something I thought you might like after your recent rise to fame!'

William couldn't help but smile, toying with the smooth jewel in his fingers, 'thanks Grandpa Rupert, but I think I've got it covered.' And with that he threw the stone into his bin, before jumping online to play his new video game; *Captain Bubblegum 3: In space no one can hear you blow*, with his friends.

And that's where the story would end, should end perhaps.

But while William's back was turned, deep within the Captain Bubblegum multiverse, Kevin, or rather Barry Fatfeathers, waddled quietly into his room, where he began pecking around in his brother's bin, sure to find half-eaten candy bars or scrunched up tissues with "tasty" bogeys inside.

But things were about to change for Kevin, and change in the most fantastic and incredible way, as his little hand began to warm, holding the sparkly green gemstone.

The End

ACKNOWLEDGEMENT

Thanks to all my wonderful friends and amazing family who have encouraged me never to give up on my dream of being a fiction writer. I know I've been going on about writing books for a long, long time, often sidetracked by paid writing jobs, but finally I've done it. Hooray!

A special thanks to my husband Jon for spell checking and reading this story to our kids so brilliantly, and thanks to my boys Elliot and Cody for enjoying it. Finally, a huge thank you to the amazingly talented Dani Dixon for bringing William to life with her incredible cover art for this book.

It takes a strange type of bravery to create something from scratch, hone it for months that become years, and eventually stick it out there for all the world to see in the hope that someone might like it too. Bravery doesn't even feel like the right word, I guess it's closer to hope. I hope some people (kids as well as any adults reading it to them) love it as much as I do. If that happens then great, and if not then that's okay too, because as Elbert Hubbard once said; "There is only one way to avoid criticism; do nothing, say nothing, and be nothing." That wasn't good enough for William and it's not good enough for me.

ABOUT THE AUTHOR

Natalie Denton

My origin story is a simple one; I wanted to be a writer. I decided that if I was to do something I truly loved, I'd never "work" a day in my life. For most of my career I'd say that has been true, having produced thousands of magazine articles, creative copy for websites and content for non-fiction books and bookazines. But while writing for other people has helped my career and paid the  bills, it's never alleviated my desire to write stories, only get in the way of that dream. But here it is, finally published, my first of many stories.

Printed in Great Britain
by Amazon